Sabrina
The Teenage Witch®

Sabrina's
Guide to the Universe

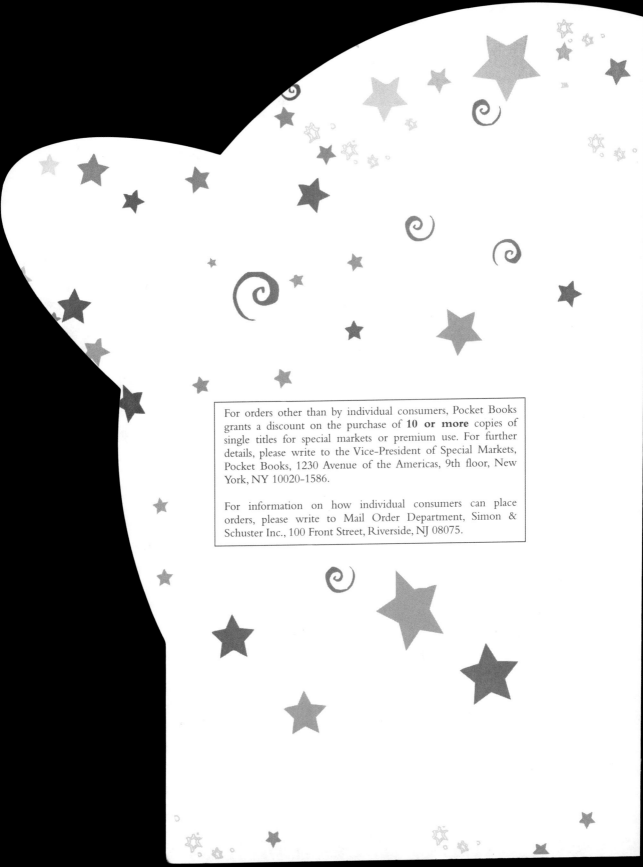

Sabrina
The Teenage Witch®

Sabrina's
Guide to the Universe

Patricia Barnes-Svarney

AN ARCHWAY PAPERBACK
Published by POCKET BOOKS
New York London Toronto Sydney Singapore

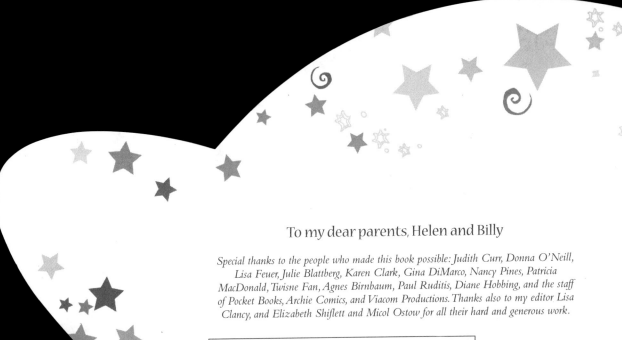

To my dear parents, Helen and Billy

Special thanks to the people who made this book possible: Judith Curr, Donna O'Neill, Lisa Feuer, Julie Blattberg, Karen Clark, Gina DiMarco, Nancy Pines, Patricia MacDonald, Twisne Fan, Agnes Birnbaum, Paul Ruditis, Diane Hobbing, and the staff of Pocket Books, Archie Comics, and Viacom Productions. Thanks also to my editor Lisa Clancy, and Elizabeth Shiflett and Micol Ostow for all their hard and generous work.

AN ARCHWAY PAPERBACK Original

An Archway Paperback published by
POCKET BOOKS, a division of Simon & Schuster, Inc.
1230 Avenue of the Americas, New York, NY 10020

ISBN: 0-671-03641-6

First Archway Paperback printing December 1999

10 9 8 7 6 5 4 3 2 1

Cover design by Lisa Litwack
Book design and composition by Diane Hobbing of Snap-Haus Graphics

Printed in the U.S.A.

Contents

Introduction

Hi! Sabrina Spellman here.

I was talking to my aunts and cat in the kitchen the other day when we came up with a great idea—to tour the universe! What's the use of being a witch if you can't use some of the perks?

After all, we're all witches. My cat, Salem, is a warlock who tried to take over the world. The Witches' Council punished him by turning him into a black cat. (At first for 100 years, and because he can't stay out of trouble, now for 150 years.) And my aunts, Zelda and Hilda, are both witches. So am I— well, I'm half mortal, half witch.

Of course, there was a good reason for *my* interest in touring the cosmos. My physics teacher gave my class a major assignment: write a paper about the universe—in a week. (Life would be so much easier if all I had to do was pull a rabbit out of my hat.)

Who, me panic? You bet! I had to discover everything about the universe in only seven days. Although I'm pretty good with a spell, it would still be hard for me to find my way through the universe all by myself.

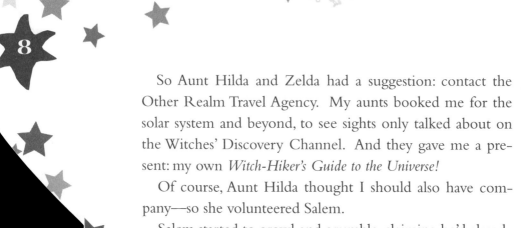

8

So Aunt Hilda and Zelda had a suggestion: contact the Other Realm Travel Agency. My aunts booked me for the solar system and beyond, to see sights only talked about on the Witches' Discovery Channel. And they gave me a present: my own *Witch-Hiker's Guide to the Universe!*

Of course, Aunt Hilda thought I should also have company—so she volunteered Salem.

Salem started to growl and grumble, claiming he'd already been there. But when I promised to let him watch his favorite television programs for two whole weeks (and let him play with the remote control), he agreed to come along. He said he was tired of watching dust float by anyway.

We want you to come along, too. So grab your backpack, brain, and this book. Here are some really cool things Salem and I found out about the magic of the universe!

One last note before we start:

Some activities may require adult supervision. Don't forget to double-check with a parent or an adult before starting any of these experiments.

Swing Around the Earth

Some days my friends call me a space cadet, but that's only when I'm thinking about a hundred other things or having a bad hair day. Other times my feet are firmly planted on the Earth—which is why I'm so partial to this planet. (Salem says Earth is his favorite planet, too. It's the only place where he gets good television reception for his favorite Cat-TV channel!)

I grabbed the map the Other Realm Travel Agency sent me. As I unfolded it, Salem sighed. "So many worlds to conquer, so little time this week."

We decided to start with the obvious: the third planet from the sun, our Earth. Sometimes it seems as if the only thing I know about the Earth is our house in Westbridge, my aunts, my friends, my high school, and the local mall. But I was in for a few "earthly" surprises.

Pulling out my *Witch-Hiker's Guide to the Universe,* I read to Salem that our planet is almost, but not quite, circular in shape. Here are a few other Earth facts:

• It has a thick blanket of air—called the atmosphere—that allows plants and animals to breathe.
• **About seventy percent of the planet is covered by the oceans**, with plenty of tuna (Salem made me say that).
• It also has seven large chunks of land called continents, and over millions of years **the continents move**—*really, really* slowly—around the planet.
• The Earth turns on its axis (rotates) every 24 hours, and travels around the sun (revolves) in 365 days—or one year.

But there were a few more things we needed to find out about the Earth.

Earth to Sabrina

*E*verything is relative. A witch-wart on my nose when I'm going to a high school dance is always too big. And the salmon "sand-witch" Salem makes for lunch is always too big.

But just how big is our planet? Salem and I decided to ask Aunt Zelda, so we popped back home.

"I have just the person," she said.

> "Hold your head, watch your knees,
> and bring us Eratosthenes!"

POOF! A short, bearded man in a long orange robe appeared.

Aunt Zelda explained that Eratosthenes was a librarian and astronomer who lived over 2,000 years ago. And although the astronomer protested—he was very shy—Aunt Zelda said that he was the first person to work out the **circumference** of—or distance around—the Earth. The circumference would be the path you'd take if you took Salem for a walk starting from Westbridge, walked in a straight line around the

world, and ended up in Westbridge again. (Salem says he'll just stick to walking from the living room to the kitchen, thank you very much.)

After stroking his beard for a while, Eratosthenes said finding the Earth's circumference was simple.

He knew the sun's light reached the bottom of a deep well in the city of Syene at 12 noon. He also had an assistant measure the angle of the sun's shadow in the city of Alexandria at the same time. Then the astronomer measured the distance between the two cities.

Based on the angles and the distance, Eratosthenes worked out that the Earth's circumference was 25,054 miles.

Salem looked it up in his *Handy Cat Encyclopedia*. He found out **the Earth's true average circumference is 24,857 miles**. Not bad considering Eratosthenes did it all without a calculator or computer!

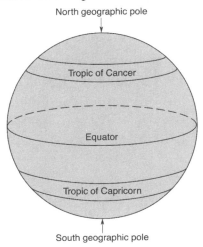

Salem Says

I suppose it's up to *me* to talk about the more exciting things about the Earth. After all, it's important to know about the planet you want to take over.

The Earth is really ancient, around 4.5 billion years old. (And I thought 150 years of being a house cat was a long time!)

I also found out our planet is layered like an onion. Hmmm . . . like a salmon smothered in onions . . . and maybe some pickles on the side . . . what was I talking about? Oh, yeah . . .

The Earth's layers start in the center, known as the inner and outer cores, then the mantle, and finally, the most important place because it's where I sit—the crust.

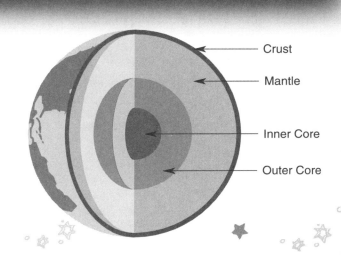

Crust

Mantle

Inner Core

Outer Core

What Winter?

Ah, winter. When every kid in Westbridge High School hopes for some snow days.

Anyway, why do we *have* spring, summer, fall, and winter? Aunt Hilda was just about to enter the linen closet when I caught up with her. She nodded and twirled a finger in the air.

Suddenly we were in Italy staring at a tall building leaning to one side. "Behold the Leaning Tower of Pisa—not to be confused with pizza," she said. She pointed to a balcony near the top of the tower. "The astronomer Galileo Galilei and I used to have some fine chats about pigeons and pasta up there."

Between bites of pasta, Galileo once explained to her that **the Earth's axis is tilted**—sort of like the building—and the planet's tilt is the reason for the seasons. It appears to lean toward the sun around June 20th, or summer in Massachusetts; then it appears to lean away from the sun around December 20th, when my friends and I wish for snow days. In between we have spring and fall. In the Southern Hemisphere—in other words, for Australian kangaroos and other creatures to the south—the seasons are just the opposite.

Funky Fact

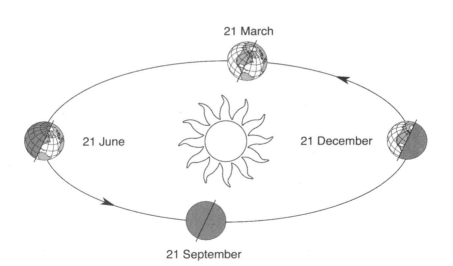

As strange as it may seem, the **Earth's orbit** takes the planet *closer* to the sun in January—when the north is freezing cold—and farther away from the sun in June, during our Massachusetts summer!

21 March

21 June

21 December

21 September

Salem Says

When I found out it takes the **Earth about 365 days to get around the sun**, I decided to figure out how many days I'll be a cat. Let's see . . . if I count on one paw . . . one . . . two . . . oh, that won't work. How about multiplying 365 days times 150 years . . . You mean I have to be a cat for 54,750 days? And what about the extra days for leap years? I demand a recount!

Cats Know Best?

You ou probably noticed that we all breathe on Earth.

My physics teacher asked us to discuss the Earth's atmosphere in our report. Salem checked his *Handy Cat Encyclopedia,* and it said: "The Earth's atmosphere is composed of 78 percent nitrogen, 21 percent oxygen, less than 1 percent argon, and the rest as traces of other gases. The atmosphere is broken into layers. We live in the bottom layer of the atmosphere called the troposphere—where all the weather takes place."

Hmmm . . . It's as if we can't decide whether we're at the bottom or on top: We live at the bottom of the atmosphere in the troposphere, but on top of the Earth at the crust.

Salem Says

I confess. I once dated Marie Curie before she found Pierre more interesting. (Her loss. It was probably for the best. She was always talking about chemistry—a beaker here, a noble gas there.) She *did* mention that a gas surrounding the Earth called ozone is made up of three molecules of oxygen rather than the usual two. This **ozone layer** is higher up than the troposphere, and protects animals and plants from the sun's harmful rays—sort of like a huge blanket of sunscreen surrounding the planet!

Earth Orbit 101

𝓘'm still trying to get the hang of my flying vacuum cleaner. And as Aunt Hilda says, practice (almost, but not quite) makes perfect. Using my magic, I flew the vacuum—with Salem sitting behind me—into the vacuum of space. We took off for Earth's orbit, following the Other Realm Travel Agency map.

We weren't the only "objects" flying around our planet. There were also hundreds of satellites, and tiny chunks of space rock. But two big objects caught our eye as we flew high above the Earth: The **Hubble Space Telescope** and the **International Space Station**.

As we passed by the wide wings of the Hubble Space Telescope's two huge solar panels, Salem grabbed my *Witch-Hiker's Guide*. "It says here that the Hubble Space Telescope was launched in 1990. And it's seen farther into the universe than anyone has ever seen—almost ten times better than telescopes on the ground. Wow! You should see the pictures. Here's one of the Cat's Eye nebula. That has to be the center of the universe . . . I just know it . . . Cats are alway at the center of important things."

I rolled my eyes (sometimes that's the only way to deal with Salem), and we flew toward the International Space Station. It looked like a giant had been playing with Tinkertoys—long grayish cylinders hooked to a bunch of flat, dark solar panels. I read in the newspaper that the astronauts will make more than 40 spacewalks to build the place, completing the station by 2005.

Hmm . . . now if only someone would start a nice Italian restaurant nearby!

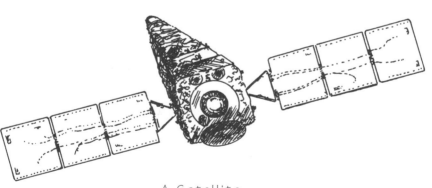

A Satellite

 Salem Says

One thing I noticed about flying above the Earth: I don't weigh as much as I do on the ground. That means I can eat as many cans of tuna or slices of pizza as I want without gaining weight—as long as I stay in space. On the Earth's surface Sabrina and I weigh a certain amount because the planet's gravity pulls on us. But in space Sabrina and I are almost **weightless** because there is little gravity. Bring on the doughnuts!

Fly Me to the Moon

*S*ince Salem is always singing to the full moon, I decided that he should find out more about our only natural satellite. (Not to mention it was a question for my physics project.)

As we flew by the **moon**, I noticed that only one side faces the Earth. The other side, called the "far side," *always* points away from the Earth. (It's like dancing with my boyfriend Harvey—no matter how much we spin, I always like to face him!)

Salem said he likes the moon because it has **phases**. When it's at the "full moon" phase, the sun lights the entire moon's face we see from Earth. When it's "new moon" phase, the moon is between the Earth and the sun—and the sun's so bright, we can't see the moon against it at all. When the moon is just a sliver, it's called the "crescent moon" phase; half-lit is the "half-moon" phase; and just over half-lit, it's called the "gibbous moon" phase. (For witches, it's important to know the phases. After all, we're not supposed to fly during a gibbous moon—the glare from the moon reduces visibility.)

Of course, this light show has an effect on the moon. Using my magic, Salem and I stood on the fully lit side and measured the temperature with a large thermometer. It was 260° F! Then we flew to the dark side, and the temperature was down to -280° F.

Funky Fact

Two spacecraft called *Clementine* and the *Lunar Prospector* recently found **evidence of ice on the moon**. Scientists believe that there may be a mix of dirt and ice crystals—especially in the large basins at the moon's south pole. In other words, one day there may be a way to water a "lunar garden!"

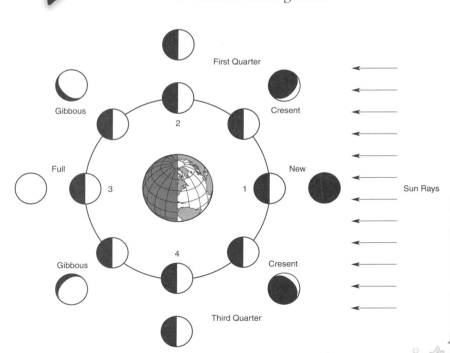

First Quarter

Gibbous

Cresent

2

Full

New

3

1

Sun Rays

Gibbous

Cresent

4

Third Quarter

Face It!

If I had a face like the moon, I'd be calling for makeup. The surface of the moon looks like a pizza I once made at the Slicery when I worked for Mrs. Popowski—one with the works, including anchovies and pepperoni. Salem thinks the moon's face looks like a jolly elf blowing out candles on a birthday cake or one of the witches on the Witches' Council who turned him into a cat.

What's the moon really like? Salem and I saw huge, dark areas and plenty of holes in the surface. I checked the *Witch-Hiker's Guide to the Universe,* and it explained what we were seeing: Apparently, astronomers long ago had bad eyesight and just as bad telescopes. So they named the regions of darker rock on the moon *mare* (Latin for "sea"), thinking the moon was filled with oceans. (Hey, even witches before the Renaissance knew that the moon had no oceans!)

The moon also has hundreds of **craters**, or big holes in the ground caused by space objects hitting the surface. And it has plains and mountain ranges, but they look very different from those on Earth. There are no people, houses, malls, streets, flowers, cats, dogs, bookstores, or trees—just rock.

All this talk about the moon makes me hungry. After all, you've probably heard the moon is made of green cheese—definitely not something I'd order in a Paris café.

What is the moon really made of? Rock, of course! And it's pretty old. In fact, of the 847 pounds of rock brought back from the moon by the Apollo astronauts, one in particular showed that **the moon is just over 4 billion years old—around the same age as the Earth.**

Boy, imagine how it would smell if it was really made of green cheese!

Make Your Own Magic in the Universe

All right. We've visited the Earth and moon so far—and there must be something you can do to view these objects a bit better. You don't need magic to see the Earth. It's right in front of you! But there is something you can do from your own backyard: Watch the moon.

All you need are binoculars or a small telescope. Even if you don't have either one, you can still use the best instrument—your eyes—to see some of the larger features on the moon on a clear night. Most of them are named after famous scientists my aunts and Salem know.

Take the crater Copernicus, named after the famous Polish astronomer, Nicolaus Copernicus (or "Nicky" to Aunt Hilda). See the darkest blobs (mares) on the moon's left side? Almost right in the center is a bright spot—the huge crater Copernicus.

Then there's the crater Tycho, named after the Danish astronomer Tycho Brahe. It's a large crater that looks like it's surrounded by bright rays—and it's what makes the southern part of the moon look so bright.

Big Guys Near Us

We had six more days to gather information about the universe. And although our next stops were close by, we needed to know more about the **inner solar system**. Sure, I knew there was the sun and a few planets, but I needed details.

"Why not contact ORIL?" Salem said.

I scratched my head and asked him what he meant.

He sighed. "The Other Realm Information Librarian," he answered. "You know, the librarian who always slaps my paws when I make slurping noises at the library's drinking fountain. *You* try hanging on with your front paws *and* pushing the button for water."

I decided he was right. Not about the drinking fountain, but about getting some help. According to my magic book, all it took was a spell:

> "Grab stacks of books and ring a bell,
> you'll conjure up the ORIL!"

A short woman with curly hair, a dark blue dress, and round glasses popped up on her own flying vacuum. She immediately reached over and slapped Salem's paw, saying "Stop that slurping!" Then she turned to me and held out her hand. "Call me Oril. All my friends do."

When I explained our problem, she was more than ready to help. The first thing she taught us was how to remember the order of the planets from the sun outward: "*Magic Violins Entertain Me Just So Ukuleles Never Play*," or **M**ercury, **V**enus, **E**arth, **M**ars, **J**upiter, **S**aturn, **U**ranus, **N**eptune, and **P**luto.

We were on our way.

Woo-hoo!

Pluto   Neptune Uranus   Saturn   Jupiter   Mars Earth Venus Mercury

Sun

Sunny Side Up

I've seen a bunch of beautiful sunsets and plenty of sunrises—especially when I stayed up all night studying for my witches' license. But it's not only sunrises and sunsets that make our **sun** so special—it also has to do with heat and light. (After all, it would be a drag without the sun. I just can't imagine my friends and I watching Harvey play football in the dark all the time!)

The sun is really a star—and it's not just something that lights up a football game. It also keeps us all warm. Without it, life on Earth wouldn't exist. In other words, it would be awful. There would be no Aunt Hilda, Aunt Zelda, Salem, Harvey, Valerie . . . Libby, Mr. Kraft . . . hmmm, I'll have to think about those two.

As we rounded the sun, Oril explained a few things. Our sun is huge—but it's still just average when compared to other stars. **The surface temperature is about 11,000° F.** This is much hotter than our average summertime temperature in Massachusetts of 75° F—and probably hotter than anything I've managed to toast in my Home Ec class!

The sun's surface also has funky-looking dots called **sunspots**—which are actually areas on the surface that are

relatively cooler than the surrounding regions. Around the sunspots are **flares**, huge twisting columns of gas that shoot high above the sun's surface. Some of the particles from the flares often head toward the Earth. And if the flares are strong enough, people who live toward the north and south poles can see an **aurora**—beautiful curtains and bursts of colored light created as the particles play with the Earth's magnetic field.

Talk about natural magic!

Salem Says

Most people immediately notice my sunny personality—except maybe Sabrina. And Hilda. And Zelda. Oh, all right. So I'm grumpy. But you would be, too, if you discovered that the sun has **only 6 billion years left** before it swells up into a red giant star. By then, I should be well on my way to taking over the universe!

Funky Fact

How many Earths—not counting people or buildings—would weigh as much as the sun? My *Witch-Hiker's Guide to the Universe* says it would take 327 magic Boliana sandworms or 333,400 Earths to weigh as much as the sun.

Catch That Planet!

There isn't much to the closest planet to the sun, **Mercury**. Salem and I noticed that the planet is covered with craters. (There's even the "Teddy Bear," three craters that look like a teddy bear, with a round face and two ears on top.) Mercury also has a few mountain ranges and plains—but with no grass, trees, or living things that we're used to on Earth—and no real atmosphere. In fact, it looks like the Earth's moon only bigger.

On a Mercury day, it can be twice the hottest setting in our kitchen oven—and seven times colder than inside our refrigerator freezer during a Mercury night.

According to Oril, the tiny planet speeds around the sun (or revolves) in only about 88 Earth-days. That makes **one Mercury year equal to only 88 Earth days.** That's pretty fast. In other words, if you were 11 Mercury-years old today, you would be just over two and a half Earth-years old. Or if you were 10 years old on Earth, you'd be 41 Mercury-years old! (Whew! Talk about a time warp.)

I'm definitely going to suggest we move Westbridge High School to Mercury. That way, when I have only six Mercury-days to write a physics paper, it would be equal to 354 Earth-days. Woo-hoo!

Funky Fact

Hot and dry Mercury may run around the sun fast, but it's a slowpoke in terms of days—or the time it takes the planet to rotate (spin) on its axis. One Mercury-day is equal to almost 59 days on Earth.

Salem Says

I happen to know **how Mercury got its name**. The guy was a friend of mine from long ago: the fleet-footed messenger of the gods named Mercury. He was always running around when you just wanted to sit and plot the takeover of the world!

Hey, Sis!

I contacted my aunts when we reached **Venus**—which is called the Earth's sister planet only because it's about the same size. Hilda and Zelda are sisters, so I figured they could tell me about the planet. No luck. Hilda warned me not to take any photos and Zelda told me not to wear blue.

Using my magic powers, Oril, Salem, and I stood on the surface. And we knew why my aunts were staying away: **The planet was hot—almost 900° F and hot enough to melt lead on the surface**. One reason is that a gas called carbon dioxide fills the air, holding in the heat like a greenhouse. Because it's so hot, there are no oceans or beaches—or life. And because the thick clouds are made of sulfuric acid, everything has a bright yellow cast. I looked horrible in that light and Oril's blue outfit looked green on Venus—at least the part that didn't melt.

But we *did* like the tall volcanic mountains, huge craters, and rounded domes on Venus—including one that looked like a giant tick on the surface. And the weirdest part was the winds in the upper level of the atmosphere that reached 225 miles per hour. (Aunt Zelda said it cuts down flight time on the witch sailplane races held there every year.)

 Salem Says

Venus is hard to miss in the Earth's nighttime sky. Depending on where it is in its orbit, our sister planet is either a bright evening star in the west at sunset, or morning star in the east at sunrise. In fact, **Venus is one of the brightest objects in the sky**, not including the sun and moon. I've heard some of my cat friends accidentally howl at Venus instead of the moon.

(Not all cats have as good eyesight as I.)

Visit to a Rusty Planet

Oril and I hopped on our flying vacuums again. We got to **Mars** in no time, thanks to my flying and the Other Realm Travel Agency map.

Mars is one of my favorite planets because it has two polar caps perfect for skiing. It's also about **half the size of the Earth** and has thin air made of mostly carbon dioxide.

But the real reason I was there this time was to see something cool: the biggest volcano in the solar system, **Olympus Mons** (it's taller than the tallest mountain on Earth, Mount Everest). Salem had been there before, but he couldn't remember if it was left or right of the Vallis Marinaris, the huge valley that cuts across a quarter of the planet. And unlike Salem, I'm willing to ask directions.

I opened my *Witch-Hiker's Guide to the Universe* and checked under "Mars." There was the spell I needed:

> "Make some jam, spread some jelly,
> then send us Mr. Schiaparelli!"

A small man with a long beard and dark brown suit popped up next to Salem and blinked. "Where am I?"

It was the great **Italian astronomer Giovanni Schiaparelli.** When I told him that he was on Mars, he said. "I must be dreaming. That will teach me to stay up so late at the opera. Oh, well, now that I'm here, want to check out some canals?"

As we walked, he explained how in 1877, Mars came closer to the Earth's orbit—within millions of miles—which, believe me, in astronomical terms is *close*. Schiaparelli used a telescope to see the planet, and he saw long lines he called *canali*. That's when his headaches began. *Canali* means "channels" in Italian, and Schiaparelli thought they were rivers carrying water from the polar ice caps. But some astronomers interpreted Schiaparelli's word as "canals"—meaning manmade structures, or, in this case, built by intelligent Martians.

I looked around and didn't see any Martians—just the two Martian moons, Phobos and Deimos, orbiting the planet. Oril explained that the "canals" are actually illusions—sort of like eye magic. Depending on the angle of the sun, the time of the year (Mars has seasons, too), and the types of rock and soil, certain areas look like straight lines from on Earth.

As we looked around, we saw long winding channels, craters, deserts, and frost. And even though Salem, Oril, Mr. Schiaparelli, and I were there on a Martian "summer"

day, it was very different from Westbridge. More like a freezing day in the Sahara desert—but without as much oxygen. We also noticed that a dust storm was coming in, complete with 200-mile-per-hour winds. As we watched, a few dust devils passed by—miles-high columns of dust churned up by the winds.

Ho, hum. Just your typical wild and crazy summer day on Mars.

Salem Says

I hate to name-drop, but I was with Orson Welles when he did the radio broadcast in 1938 of *The War of the Worlds,* a fiction novel by H. G. Wells (no relation). What a panic—literally! Listeners who heard the broadcast believed that the Earth was *really* being invaded by **Martians**!

But I also know there may be real Martians. Scientists are trying to agree if some meteorites that fell to the Earth from space have Martian fossils inside.

Wow!

Move over, Mr. Wells and Mr. Welles!

Funky Fact

"Greetings, Martians!" is what they would say if they could talk: There, sitting on a dry, rocky plain on the planet Mars are the *Pathfinder* craft and its little rover, the *Sojourner*, the latest **spacecraft from Earth to the planet Mars**. These two craft took some of the best pictures of the Martian surface in 1997. And there's also the *Mars Global Surveyor*. This craft took some of the neatest pictures of the planet, too—from high in orbit—starting in 1998. (The ultimate tourists, they also took pictures of each other!)

Make Your Own Magic in the Universe

You don't have to be as smart as Aunt Zelda to figure out how to make your own version of the **greenhouse planet Venus.** All you need is a small plastic bag, two eight- to twelve-inch sticks, a rubber band, a small potted plant, and a sunny window. Water the soil or potted plant so it's just damp—not soggy or dry. Then place the two sticks in the soil and put the plastic bag over the sticks. Use the rubber band to hold the plastic around the pot. Then put the pot in the sunshine—and wait.

This may not be exactly what it's like on Venus. After all, the cloudy planet has no water or plants. But you are creating a greenhouse effect: The sun heats up the inside of the plastic bag, causing the water or plant to release water vapor. That's the water collecting on the inside of the bag. After about a half day in the sunshine, stick your hand quickly inside. Do you notice how hot it is in the bag? This is because the plastic bag traps the heat of the sun inside—a miniature greenhouse effect.

If you ever visit a large greenhouse, you'll notice the same effect: The glass lets in the heat and holds most of it there.

On Venus the heat from the sun reaches through the clouds to the surface but can't escape.

Just be glad your greenhouse doesn't heat up as much as the surface of Venus. Take it from me—there's no air-conditioning on the planet!

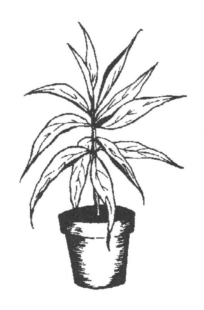

Big Guys Far Away

By the time Salem and I reached some of the biggest planets in the solar system, Oril was fast asleep. (Salem said there's an old saying in the Other Realm: "Let sleeping information librarians lie." I think he just wanted her breakfast.)

When I looked over my notes for physics class and the Other Realm Travel Agency map, I knew we needed some help—and some extra magic. After all, the next planets in the **outer solar system** were the biggest. There was so much to learn. We were off again!

What? No Surface?

I contacted Aunt Zelda and said we were trying to land the flying vacuum on **Jupiter**—and apparently we needed help!

She immediately told us we couldn't stand on Jupiter—because **it has no real surface.** It's really just a ball of colorful, moving gases such as hydrogen, helium, and methane. (Sort of a crystal ball on overload.)

"Wait. I know someone who can help. . . . Abracadabra!" Aunt Zelda said, then stopped, pointed, and said:

> "We won't cry and we won't mope,
> just bring us Galileo and his telescope!"

Beards must have always been the "in" look for famous astronomers. There stood a bearded man in a seventeenth-century white-collared outfit, holding a small telescope. We explained to the great astronomer and philosopher where he was—on the giant planet Jupiter. Galileo didn't seem to mind. He said he'd seen stranger things in his telescope.

Galileo told us he first turned his telescope—and it wasn't much more powerful than an average pair of binoculars today—on Jupiter in January 1610. That's when he noticed four strange "stars" around the planet. They turned out to be four large moons around Jupiter—Callisto, Ganymede, Io, and Europa—now named the **Galilean satellites**. Galileo seemed very proud to learn that the moons were named after him. (I bet Galileo would also be proud to know there was a spacecraft named after him currently orbiting the giant planet—*if* he knew what a spacecraft was!)

Galileo didn't know much more. He started looking around for Aunt Hilda, his pasta date from the Leaning Tower of Pisa. We sent him back to Westbridge, then I grabbed Salem and my flying vacuum and did some measurements of my own.

Do you want to see the definition of *big*? Jupiter is it. I already knew it was the fifth planet from the sun and the largest planet in the solar system. When I conjured up a giant ruler to measure the planet, I found out that it makes the Earth look puny: **It's about 11 times the Earth's diameter**.

The planet also has tight, swirling masses of gas that are actually huge storms. In fact, there is one storm on the planet called the **Great Red Spot** that has lasted for more than 300 years. (No witch has yet claimed responsibility!)

There are also "no flying vacuums zones for witches" at the equator—because the winds can reach up to 360 miles per hour.

I think I'll stick to flying over Westbridge!

Salem Says

I don't know if you were invited to the great cosmic fireworks back in July 1994. (I was, of course.) That's when pieces of the **comet Shoemaker-Levy 9** smashed into the planet Jupiter going about 134,000 miles per hour!

It was quite a sight from Earth. Sabrina wasn't with us yet, but there was Hilda in a party hat, Zelda setting up the telescope, me in my burgundy cummerbund . . . and the comet pieces hitting the planet—each looking like a flash of fireworks!

Many Moons

Jupiter has a bunch of **moons** around it. No one knows the exact number because scientists are always discovering more—but as we flew by, I counted 16.

Salem and I dipped closer to the Galilean moons Europa, Ganymede, and Callisto—all ice-covered moons. We also flew by Io—a moon hotter than a cat on a hot tin roof (no offense to Salem). We spotted at least nine active volcanoes on the moon throwing hot sulfur into the sky, making it smell like rotten eggs. It's being pulled by Jupiter's gravity, making the moon heat up from all the friction.

And I thought the Slicery was a hot spot!

Salem Says

I know a few more things about the Galilean moon **Europa**. (Maybe I'll tell Sabrina for a few jars of herring in cream sauce.) I heard there may be an ocean under Europa's icy surface, which means there could be primitive forms of life on the moon. (More creatures to conquer!) But we're talking *small* here—almost the size of bacteria. . . . Hmmm . . . I wonder if they could follow simple directions, like "feed Salem now"?

Saturn Ear Rings

We were ready to head for our next destination: the **ringed planet Saturn**. Aunt Zelda returned Galileo to his own century because he was tired of hearing the same old story: Yes, he saw the rings in his telescope centuries ago. And yes, he thought the rings were actually handles on the planet! (He explained it was tough to get a good telescope back then.)

After we said goodbye to Aunt Zelda, Salem and I hopped on my flying vacuum. Salem decided it was time to wake Oril up. The librarian looked around groggily. "Please state your question in thirty words or less. . . . Sorry, I thought I was back in the Other Realm Library. Where are we? Oh, that's right—on to Saturn!"

We were circling the planet in no time. But what about some details? Taking out our ruler again, we found out the ringed planet is the second largest in the solar system—**nine times the diameter of the Earth**. Its air is mostly hydrogen, and it has more than 20 moons. (Again, scientists are discovering more all the time.)

Did you know **Saturn's rings** are actually thousands of rings no more than a few hundred feet thick? (In fact, the

ridges and grooves look like the huge records my aunts used to play on something called a record player.) From where we were, Saturn's beautiful rings sparkled and reflected sunlight. They're really made up of dirty snowball-like chunks of ice, ranging in size from small specks to large boulders.

"And you would also have a hard time getting your homework done on Saturn and Jupiter, young lady," Oril said, looking over her glasses. "They both spin around on their axes in about 10 hours. On Earth it takes 24 hours." Then she winked out of sight.

Now, *that* made my head spin.

Funky Fact

Scientists are hoping to learn more about Saturn in the early 2000s. That's when a small spacecraft called **Cassini** will orbit and start taking measurements of the planet's surface and rings. It's also going to drop an even smaller spacecraft—the *Huygens*—into the swirling gases of the planet.

Salem Says

When I was a witch, I had lots of fun in the bathtub! First I'd bring in my rubber ducky. Then, my favorite sailboat. But at that time, I didn't know about the ultimate floating toy, the planet Saturn. Why? Because Saturn is made up of so many light gases, **it would float in water**.

Yes, I can see it now. I'd be the ruler of the planet Saturn! (Of course, I'd also have to find a tub big enough for the planet to float in.)

Make Your Own Magic in the Universe

How old would you be on any of the planets in the solar system?

One way to discover this "planetary magic" is to determine how many days you've been on Earth. For example, if you were ten years old today, you would have been around for 3,652 Earth-days. (That's 10 x 365, plus 2 extra days for leap years.) Figure out how old you are on the other planets by dividing that number by the number of Earth-days that planet takes to get around the sun.*

For Mercury, divide 3,652 by 87.97. That equals about 41 Mercury-years old!

* If you aren't sure exactly how many days old you are, round off to the nearest year.

One Planet-Year (in Earth Days)		*For example, 10 years old on Earth:*
Mercury	87.97	41 Mercury-years old
Venus	224.7	16 Venus-years old
Earth	365.2	10 Earth-years old
Mars	686.98	5 Martian-years old
Jupiter	4,330.6	less than a Jupiter-year old
Saturn	10,747	less than a Saturn-year old
Uranus	30,588	less than a Uranus-year old
Neptune	59,800	less than a Neptune-year old
Pluto	90,591	less than a Pluto-year old

Neighbors at the End of the Block

The next day I grabbed the Other Realm Travel Agency map and headed out farther into the solar system toward **Uranus** and **Neptune**. Suddenly Aunt Zelda appeared on her flying vacuum.

I was glad to see my aunt. After all, she has access to her lab-top where she can make some great spells and concoctions. Not only that, she knew the guys who discovered Uranus and Neptune.

She cast a spell for us:

> "Skip the show, skip the commercial,
> we'll just settle for William Herschel!"

Apparently, by the 1800s, beards were out for astronomers—but not tight collars. A man with white hair, a long black overcoat, and a tie around his tight collar appeared on the back of Aunt Zelda's vacuum.

The British musician and amateur astronomer Herschel told us that his discovery of the planet **Uranus** was accidental. He was actually just looking at the stars through his telescope one night in March 1781 when he saw what he thought was a comet. A few months later he realized it was a planet—and he was an instant celebrity. At first he named this third largest planet Star of George (Georgium Sidus) in honor of King George II of Great Britain. Then it was called Herschel in his honor. Eventually, someone suggested the name Uranus, after the mythological father of Saturn—and it stuck.

I was pleased. Can you imagine remembering the name Georgium Sidus instead of Uranus?

I noticed that Uranus isn't all that bad for a planet. It has the **brightest clouds** in the outer solar system. I counted 18 moons—all named after characters in William Shakespeare plays. And more moons are being discovered all the time. (Did you hear they found another moon around Uranus in 1999?) Astronomers have identified at least 11 different

rings—not as bright or large as Saturn's—that wobble like an unbalanced wagon wheel for some strange reason.

Aunt Zelda suggested that we gather up the picnic basket and come back to Uranus in 2007. That's when the sun will be right over the planet's equator—and the crystals of methane are so beautiful that time of the Uranus-year. (Of course, we should also bring our parkas because it will be a bit chilly—about -300° F!)

Salem Says

Uranus also must have had a major accident in the past. (Hey—I didn't do it!) Anyway, something big—like a moon—probably hit the planet millions of years ago. Now it **spins on its side** one complete rotation about every 17 hours, like a ball.

But I didn't do it. Honest! It's not my fault!

Scooters in Space

We were ready for **Neptune** now. Aunt Zelda sent Mr. Herschel back to his own century. Then she swirled her finger three times.

> "Check the grocery, check the mall,
> and find me Mr. Johann Galle!"

Johann Galle was a small man, with sloping shoulders, white hair, and a stern look (it must have been *his* tight collar). He explained that two other astronomers, John Couch Adams and Urbain Leverrier, independently—and using math, not computers!—predicted that another planet was being gravitationally pulled by Uranus, but they didn't bother to look for it. Leverrier finally contacted Galle in 1846 and asked him to search a certain spot in the sky with a telescope. *Voila!* In less than an hour Mr. Galle said he found Neptune.

Salem and I gathered the rest of the information I needed as we circled the planet on my flying vacuum. Neptune's greenish-blue color, like on Uranus, is from methane gases in the air. The planet spins (rotates) pretty fast, about once every 16 Earth-hours. Neptune's atmosphere is dotted with

long-term storms—with names like the "Scooter" and the "Great Dark Spot," a storm almost like Jupiter's Great Red Spot but half the size. And we could just make out the planet's thin rings.

Neptune also has 8 moons—Naiad, Thalassa, Despina, Galatea, Larissa, Proteus, Triton, and Nereid—with the possibility of more being discovered every day. Triton even has a huge, cool pink (really!) polar cap and weird erupting nitrogen geysers!

Care to Go Skating?

Pluto was the last planet to visit—and the smallest in the solar system. I could tell that it would be a great place to hold the winter Olymp-witch Games. It's so cold there, the games could go on for an entire Pluto-year—it revolves around the sun once every 248 Earth years—plenty of time to get in even the stranger sports like curling and cafeteria-tray sledding. Skating would be interesting on the colorful nitrogen and methane ice fields. Because the planet is about **two-thirds the size of our own moon,** and the mostly methane atmosphere is thin, javelin and discus throws would be more exciting. Participants could actually throw objects into orbit!

Hmmm . . . I wonder if I can start an event called the "Libby-in-orbit" toss?

 *Salem Says*

I didn't want to tell Sabrina, but there may be complications to the Olymp-witch Games on the planet Pluto: Some scientists don't think Pluto *is* a planet! They think Pluto may be a former moon of Neptune, knocked out of orbit by a large space object. Not me. Planet Pluto rules!

Make Your Own Magic in the Universe

We've already figured out how old you would be on the planets in the solar system. But what about **your weight**? Here is some more "planetary magic" you can figure out on your own. Multiply your weight by the key number in this chart for each planet to find out how much you would weigh on that planet.

For example, if you weigh 100 pounds on the Earth, you would multiply 100 times the planetary number to the right. For Mars, you would weigh 38 pounds; on Jupiter, 234! Now try your own weight:

Planet	Number	Example of a 100-pound person on Earth
Mercury	0.284	28.4 pounds on Mercury
Venus	0.91	91.0 pounds on Venus
Earth	1.00	100.0 pounds on Earth
Mars	0.38	38.0 pounds on Mars
Jupiter	2.34	234.0 pounds on Jupiter
Saturn	0.925	92.5 pounds on Saturn
Uranus	0.795	79.5 pounds on Uranus
Neptune	1.125	112.5 pounds on Neptune
Pluto	0.041	4.1 pounds on Pluto

Extra:

Io, Jupiter moon	0.183	18.3 pounds on Io
Europa, Jupiter moon	0.135	13.5 pounds on Europa
Amalthea, Jupiter moon	0.007	0.7 pound on Amalthea

* Hey, do you wonder why you weigh less on larger planets like Uranus and Neptune than on Earth? My *Witch-Hiker's Guide to the Universe* had the answer: Those two planets are mostly gas, so there is less gravity. Whew! I thought I was getting spacey!

Smaller Stuff

While I was trying to see what else I needed for my physics paper, Salem was putting his paw print and a stamp on postcards. One to Aunt Zelda. One to Aunt Hilda. One to me. One to the cat down the street. One to an old girlfriend. And the list goes on. It's amazing he can take time to send so many postcards, and I can't get him to answer the phone back home.

I may be able to do plenty of magic spells, but when it comes to the magic of the universe, my spells seem lame. There were so many more things to see: bright **comets**, tumbling **asteroids**, and flashing **meteors**. And there are strange icy rocks just hanging outside the solar system.

The little guys of the universe were getting to be a big problem. It was time to call Oril again!

Rocky Belts

Oril popped up on her flying vacuum with her nose in a book. "You rang?"

I told her about our next search, and she twirled the book in the air.

> "Skip the basil and tomatoes,
> just bring on the ultimate potato!"

There, in front of us, was a huge potato-shaped chunk of rock. Oril said it was Ida, an **asteroid** from the asteroid belt, a region of space between the orbits of Mars and Jupiter containing hundreds of these chunky rocks.

Ida was dark and dusty, with huge chunks scooped out of its surface from hitting other asteroids in the belt. As we hopped on the rock, Salem almost floated off—the small asteroid doesn't have much gravitational pull. In other words, if I jumped into the air from the surface of the asteroid, I'd drift away. Cool!

Oril told us that not all asteroids are so well-behaved. There are some that have strayed from the pack in the asteroid belt.

In fact, many asteroids come close to the Earth and some even hit our planet. Around fifty thousand years ago, an asteroid half the size of a football field crash-landed in the desert of Arizona. That "small" rock blew a one-quarter-mile hole in the surface of the Earth, at a place we now call Meteor Crater.

Some scientists also believe that a huge asteroid—or many—struck the Earth 65 million years ago, long before even Salem was born. If it's true, the damage it caused could have wiped out the dinosaurs, the large and small reptiles that used to stomp around on the planet.

So *that's* why I don't see a *Tyrannosaurus rex* on my way to school—thank goodness!

Catch a Falling Star

Just what is a falling star? I grabbed the *Witch-Hiker's Guide to the Universe* and looked under "falling star." These small pieces of rock are called **meteors**—space rocks that are much smaller than asteroids—from as large as a grain of sand to the size of a big boulder. As they drop from space and enter our atmosphere, they burn up from the friction—creating beautiful streaks across the sky.

If they're big enough and land on the Earth, they are called **meteorites**. They're really impossible to catch—and if you did, you'd probably get a fistful of hot rock. *Not* cool!

Salem Says

I don't like to take a shower—most cats don't. But there is one shower I like to bask in: a **meteor shower**, mostly because there's no water involved. Several times a year the Earth travels through a bunch of old, broken-up comets. When we pass through the small rocks, we have a meteor shower. Sometimes you can see up to 100 "falling stars" per hour. It's like my own personal fireworks display!

Dirty Snowballs

There's nothing like a snowball fight. You grab a handful of snow, shape it into a ball—then throw it at Salem!

For the ultimate in snowballs, there are **comets**. Astronomers once referred to these flying space objects as dirty snowballs. Now they call them muddy snowballs. Either way, they're made of rock, dust, ice, and gases, and have been around for billions of years. They periodically travel through the solar system—swinging past the sun in an orbit or flying out of the solar system never to be seen again.

Take for instance the **comet Hale-Bopp**. You may have seen it: It showed up in the nighttime sky in 1997—looking like a bright, fuzzy dot. As it spun around the sun, our star heated up and burned off dust and gases from the comet. Particles from the sun called the solar wind pushed out the dust and gases—and the comet began to "grow" a tail, sort of like Salem's, but not as bushy.

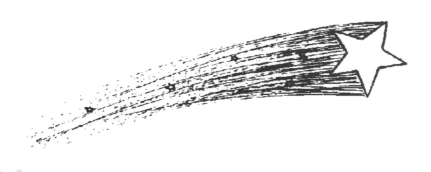

Salem Says

What's in a name? A Salem by any other name would be as wonderful . . . well, maybe.

Speaking of names, did you know they usually **name comets** after the discoverer? For example, comet Hale-Bopp was named after the two people who discovered the comet (independently and at the same time): astronomer Alan Hale and amateur astronomer Thomas Bopp.

I'd better get out there and find a comet. Comet Salem has a nice ring to it, don't you think?

Funky Fact

What famous comet keeps visiting the Earth? Salem helped me with this one. After all, he's seen the comet many times over the years. It's **comet Halley**, named by Edmond Halley who first recorded it in 1682. The comet keeps showing up about every 75 years just like clockwork whether we want to see it or not (just like how Libby shows up whenever I'm with Harvey, whether I want her to or not). The last time comet Halley gave us a view was in 1986; the next time will be in 2061.

Far Out, Dude!

Oril decided to say good-bye. She'd had enough traveling around for the day and didn't like to get too far away from our solar system. Just before she left, she told us to beware of the "little guys." I wasn't sure if she was talking about trolls or some shorter cousins I don't know about.

She shook her head and leaned close to my left ear. "No, it's them. The Kuipers," she whispered, shivering. And then she disappeared.

Salem shrugged. I shrugged. Must be some neighbors she didn't like?

As we reached **the edge of our solar system,** there stood dozens of huge rocks ahead of us.

I whipped out my *Witch-Hiker's Guide to the Universe.* The huge rocks were . . . the **Kuiper belt objects**.

These rocks surrounding our solar system are a mix of comets and asteroids. As if they can't make up their minds. Some people think the objects are the source of many of the comets that visit the solar system. And some people think the planet Pluto may be a former Kuiper belt object. Salem thinks they're all just mixed up.

Make Your Own Magic in the Universe

It's not too hard to **make a comet**. After all, it's a mix of ice and dirt—a sort of muddy snowball. If it's winter, you can make a comet outside. All you need is a mixture of half snow, one quarter ice, and one quarter dirt. If it's summer, you'll need to chop some ice from the freezer (have an adult help you) and some dirt from the yard. Just mix the two together—and you have a miniature version of a comet. (But look quickly—they melt fast!)

The real ones are a bit different. **The heart of the comet is the nucleus,** or the dirty snowball you just made. Most of the time, the comet stays frozen. But if it gets close to the sun, melting particles form **a tail.**

You won't be able to do that with your comet, but it's interesting that something as simple as ice and rock has been around the solar system for billions of years!

What Else Is Out There?

Now that Salem and I had found out everything we could about our solar system, it was time to expand our horizons. Aunt Zelda and Aunt Hilda had suggested we try the other realm—not the Other Realm in our linen closet upstairs in our house, but the area far **beyond the solar system**.

My aunts decided to join us on the last part of the trip. I started to protest as they pulled up on their flying vacuums. (I mean, can you imagine meeting up with some famous star with your aunts tagging along? Yikes!) But Aunt Hilda assured me they wouldn't cramp my style.

Of course, Aunt Zelda couldn't resist some extra help.

> "When we talk of space and time,
> then send us Albert Einstein."

The famous scientist appeared on the back of Aunt Zelda's vacuum. He looked around and ran his hand through his

tousled white hair. "Whew. I'd think I'd better check that new toothpaste I've been using."

With Salem whining that distant travel gave him a hair-ball—we were off to the stars!

Twinkle, Twinkle, Not-So-Little Star

I think Salem got too excited when Aunt Hilda said we were off to visit to some famous **stars**. You know him. He thought we were headed for Hollywood. Me? I would prefer 'N Sync—but that's another story.

Where we *did* go was out to the real stars—those mostly bright, hot balls of gas that fill the nighttime sky. There are billions and billions of stars, as the famous astronomer Carl Sagan once said. That makes our star—the sun—one in billions and billions.

Just what is a star? Mr. Einstein had the answer. He told me that stars may just look like pinpoints of light from the Earth, but they're really **big engines of gas**. And the differences between the stars are many: The coolest stars glow the reddest, while the hotter stars are yellow and white. The really, really hot stars are blue-white. Our own sun is a yellow star. One star, called Arcturus in the constellation of Boötes, is a red giant—about 25 times the diameter of our sun!

Hot stuff!

 *Salem Says*

Don't tell Sabrina, but sometimes I get confused with all these stars. It's like trying to keep track of all my cans of salmon when there's a sale at the Other Realm Grocery.

I'm not the only one. Centuries ago people needed a way to keep track of the stars in the sky. So they did what any normal mortal would do: They turned the sky into one great big connect-the-dots puzzle in the sky—called **constellations**. The constellations represented some part of mythology, and today we recognize 88 of them in our sky—from Taurus, the bull to Cygnus, the swan. My favorite is the constellation Lynx, the cat—of course!

Super Stars

*M*r. Einstein explained that stars (like mortals) all go through a **life cycle**. And they (the stars, not mortals) often go out with a bang.

What often happens is the star expands into a **red giant.** For some millions of years more, the star's core changes and begins to shrink. The end comes as the outer layer of the star blows off and drifts away into space, forming a huge smoke ring around the central core. These are called **planetary nebulae**—because they look like a planet's disk when viewed in the telescope.

That wasn't all. Aunt Zelda brought out her portable lab-top and gave everyone safety goggles. Throwing in some star chunks and particles from a gas cloud, there was another stellar surprise: the **supernova**—a massive explosion of an old star.

Aunt Hilda said she remembered a supernova from back in 1054—in a place we now call the Crab Nebula. She was visiting some Chinese astronomers looking for some nice fans for the living room when they all started talking excitedly about a "guest star." She thought they meant the Chinese emperor at first. But when she looked into the sky, a star flared up—bright enough to be visible in daylight for 23 days!

Salem Says

Hilda isn't the only one who's seen a stellar celebration. I saw a star blow up when I was partying down in Australia once: a supernova near the Tarantula Nebula in 1987—the only one seen in recent times. But the supernova was pretty far away and happened a long time ago. In fact, it took 400 years for the supernova's light to reach us in '87. Oh, well . . . *that* party's over by now!

Who Turned Out the Lights?

Of course, Mr. Einstein held back the best for last. "When is a hole not a hole?"

I scratched my head. "I give up. When is a hole not a hole?" I asked, hoping it was not going to be on my final.

He smiled. "When it's a **black hole!**"

Mr. Einstein pointed to the sky and began to explain why I didn't see anything. This was the area of a black hole—once a huge star, more than three times the mass of our own sun. Gravity shrank the star until it seemed to vanish from sight. But what really happened? The gravity was so strong, no light escaped.

I thought I might catch Mr. Einstein on this one: How do we know there are black holes out there if we can't see them? X-ray vision? Not likely! Mr. Einstein says that black holes can only be detected by the movement of other stars. The black holes have so much gravitational pull, they tug on the smaller stars nearby—and astronomers detect the tugging with delicate instruments on their telescopes. (Just as observers once *predicted* the existence of Neptune before they actually found the planet with their telescope.)

We backed up, trying not to get too close. Even Salem hid behind Aunt Zelda. Who wants to live in a black hole when there's so much shopping to be done?

Pick a Planet

When Salem's not in trouble, he's usually hungry. And even though I told him to pack enough food for our trip, he didn't listen. It's pretty empty between the stars, so I checked the Other Realm Travel Agency's map, and we headed for one of the distant planets—called **extrasolar planets** by astronomers. The plan was simple: Salem would look for something to eat, and I would look for a place to shop for something "far out" (of course!) for my friend Valerie.

We all headed for the closest planet known outside our solar system, a place around the star **51 Pegasi,** in the constellation Pegasus. According to my *Witch-Hiker's Guide to the Universe,* it's the same as the black holes: We can't see planets outside our own solar system, but we can tell they're there from observing the wobbling of nearby stars.

So far, scientists have found more than a dozen extrasolar planets. (Now if they could only figure out a way of getting a good mall up there in the 51 Pegasi's solar system!)

Funky Fact

I discovered that Aunt Hilda's cellular phone won't work at 51 Pegasi. First, we're too far from Earth. And second, because **sound travels even slower than the speed of light**—it would take thousands of years for my voice to reach the Earth from here. I'll have to stick with magic!

Spinning Dizzy

Just looking at our next destination made me a bit dizzy. There in front of us were hundreds of spinning **galaxies**, or groupings of stars that dot the universe. And they come in a number of crazy shapes and sizes. Some look like whirlpools, the antennae of an insect, blobs, and even sombreros!

I checked my *Witch-Hiker's Guide to the Universe* for this one. It said that one of the more beautiful galactic sights is our own galaxy, the **Milky Way**—seen as a long strip of stars stretching across the Northern Hemisphere's nighttime summer sky from Earth. The "milkiness" is actually the huge number of stars—sort of like trying to look through a watery glass of skim milk spilled by some magic spell that didn't go well. (We won't name names, will we, Salem Saberhagen?)

Salem Says

Sure. All of this is fine. But I want to know the big picture—like just **how big is the universe** I'm destined to rule?

I asked Albert Einstein, but he didn't know. I looked in Sabrina's *Witch-Hiker's Guide*. Nada. I asked Zelda and Hilda. I was even going to go ask Drell when Sabrina stopped me with the answer:

No one really knows.

All I know is that the universe is really, really, really big. That's fine with me. We rulers of the universe like big. It makes it easier to spread out!

Make Your Own Magic in the Universe

You can watch the stars—and even get to know the constellations, too. There are books on the constellations in your school or local library and at bookstores.

One thing you have to know is directions. Find out which way is north, south, east, and west from your backyard. Then grab a book on the constellations and start looking for the brightest stars and patterns in the sky.

For example, the brightest star in the our sky, Sirius, is found in the late autumn, winter, and early spring nighttime sky. It is not overhead, but closer to the southern horizon in most places in North America. If you find a star like Sirius, you may be able to find other stars. Just use Sirius as your "base" star—and work your way around the sky from there.

Another way to discover the constellations is to visit a local observatory or join an astronomy club (or even start one of your own at school). This way you can talk to others who may know how to find the constellations. Sometimes they have "star parties"—a cool way to check out stars and planets with a telescope and learn about the stars in our universe.

POOF! We're Back!

With a wave of her arm, Aunt Hilda landed us back in our kitchen in Westbridge. And things went back to normal in a flash.

Aunt Hilda went off to buy a new outfit.

Aunt Zelda went off with Mr. Einstein to invent a new pistachio-pineapple flavored frozen yogurt on her lab-top.

I had tons of paper to go through, lots of photos, and plenty to write about for my physics paper. I even had a day left to write it!

And of course, Salem did what any good cat would do after the mind-expanding experience of traveling to the edge of the galaxy and beyond: He dragged over his favorite pillow, plopped down on the couch, dipped into a big container of tuna packed in spring water, and turned on the Cat Channel. (They don't call him couch-potato cat for nothing.)

We hope you enjoyed the trip with us. Do you want to know more? Dig into more books on astronomy. And enjoy your own magical ride through this really cool universe!

Gotta go!

— *Sabrina*

About the Author

Patricia Barnes-Svarney first looked through a telescope at age seven, and it was love at first sight. From there, her parents bought her a telescope—and she read all the books she could find on astronomy. With her trusty English bulldog (Buff) by her side, Barnes-Svarney searched the universe, "discovering" planets, stars, and sundry space objects from her backyard—and dreaming about what it would be like to be in space. She taught astronomy for a while; now she writes nonfiction science books and articles—many on astronomy—and science fiction (in which she makes up what it would be like to be in space). She is the author of *Sabrina, The Teenage Witch: Magic Handbook*, and her fiction credits include books from the series *The Secret World of Alex Mack, Star Trek: Starfleet Academy,* and *Salem's Tails.* She's also into hiking, herb gardening, rock and fossil hunting, and birding. She lives in Endwell, New York, with her husband and assorted wild animals that eat too many peanuts.

YOU AND A FRIEND COULD WIN A TRIP TO THE KENNEDY SPACE CENTER VISITOR COMPLEX TO SEE A REAL SPACE SHUTTLE LAUNCH!

NO PURCHASE NECESSARY

Sabrina The Teenage Witch®

1 Grand Prize: A 3-day/2-night trip for three (winner plus friend and a parent or legal guardian) to see a space shuttle launch at the Kennedy Space Center Visitor Complex in Florida. Prize also Includes a Sabrina, The Teenage Witch CD-ROM; a Sabrina, The Teenage Witch hand-held game; and a Sabrina, The Teenage Witch diary kit.

Alternate grand prize: In the event that the grand prize is unavailable, the following prize will be substituted: An Overnight Group Adventure at Apollo/Saturn V Center for three (winner plus friend and a parent or legal guardian). Winner and group will sleep under the Apollo/Saturn V rocket after an evening of space-related activities, including a Kennedy Space Center Visitor Complex group bus tour, pizza party dinner, a visit with Robot Scouts, and hands-on activities. Winner and group will get a special NASA briefing of upcoming launches, demonstrations of Newton's Laws of Motion, midnight snack, breakfast, and 3-D IMAX film. Prize includes a commemorative certificate for each group and patch for each participant.

10 First Prizes: A Sabrina, The Teenage Witch Book Library consisting of: *Sabrina, The Teenage Witch, Showdown at the Mall; Good Switch, Bad Switch; Halloween Havoc; Santa's Little Helper; Ben There, Done That; All You Need is a Love Spell; Salem on Trial; A Dog's Life; Lotsa Luck; Prisoner of Cabin 13; All That Glitters; Go Fetch; Spying Eyes; Harvest Moon; Now You See Her, Now You Don't; Eight Spells a Week; I'll Zap Manhattan; Shamrock Shenanigans; The Age of Aquariums; Prom Time; Witchopoly; Bridal Bedlam; Scarabian Nights; While the Cat's Away; Fortune Cookie Fox; Haunts in the House; Up, Up, and Away; Millennium Madness; Switcheroo; Sabrina Goes to Rome; Magic Handbook;* and *Down Under.*

20 Second Prizes: A Sabrina, The Teenage Witch gift package including a Sabrina, The Teenage Witch hand-held game, a Sabrina, The Teenage Witch diary kit, and a Sabrina, The Teenage Witch CD-ROM.

50 Third Prizes: A one-year Sabrina comic books subscription and a Sabrina, The Teenage Witch diary kit.

AN ARCHWAY PAPERBACK

KENNEDY SPACE CENTER
VISITOR COMPLEX

TIGER
ELECTRONICS, LTD.

Pastime
#1 IN KIDS FUN!™

www.archiecomics.com

VIACOM
CONSUMER PRODUCTS
LICENSING DIVISION FOR *Paramount Pictures*

Knowledge Adventure
SIMON & SCHUSTER

Complete entry form and send to:
Pocket Books/ "Sabrina, The Teenage Witch Space Launch Sweepstakes"
1230 Avenue of the Americas, 13th Floor, NY, NY 10020

Name_____Birthdate___/___/___

Address_____

City_____State____Zip_____

Phone (____) _____

See below for official rules

Pocket Books/ "Sabrina, The Teenage Witch Space Launch Sweepstakes"
Sponsors Official Rules:

1. No Purchase Necessary.

2. Enter by mailing this completed Official Entry Form (no copies allowed) or by mailing a 3" x 5" card with your name and address, daytime telephone number and birthdate to the Pocket Books/ "Sabrina, The Teenage Witch Space Launch Sweepstakes", 1230 Avenue of the Americas, 13th Floor, NY, NY 10020, or to obtain a copy of these rules, write to Pocket Books/ "Sabrina, The Teenage Witch Space Launch Sweepstakes" Rules, 1230 Avenue of the Americas, 13th Floor, NY, NY 10020. Entry forms and rules are available in the back of Archway Paperbacks' Sabrina, The Teenage Witch books: *Sabrina's Guide to the Universe* (12/99), *Millennium Madness* (1/00), *Switcheroo* (3/00), and on in-store book displays. Sweepstakes begins December 1, 1999. Entries must be postmarked by April 30, 2000 and received by May 15, 2000. Sponsors are not responsible for lost, late, damaged, stolen, illegible, mutilated, incomplete, postage-due or misdirected or not delivered entries or mail or for typographical errors in the entry form or rules. Entries are void if they are in whole or in part illegible, incomplete or damaged. Enter as often as you wish, but each entry must be mailed separately. Winners will be selected at random from all eligible entries received in a drawing to be held on or about May 25, 2000. The grand-prize winner must be available to travel during the months of September and October 2000. Winners will be notified by mail. The grand-prize winner will be notified by telephone as well.

3. **Prizes: One Grand Prize:** A 3-day/2-night trip for three (winner plus a friend and a chaperone—chaperone must be winner's parent or legal guardian) to Florida including round-trip coach/economy airfare from major U.S. or U.K. airport nearest the winner's residence, round-trip ground transportation to and from airport, double-occupancy hotel accommodations and all meals ($35/pounds per person, per day). Prize does not include transfers, gratuities and any other expenses not specifically listed herein. Travel and accommodations subject to availability; certain restrictions apply. Prize also includes a Sabrina, The Teenage Witch CD-ROM (approx. retail value $29.99) from *Havas/SSI;* a Sabrina, The Teenage Witch hand-held Game (Approx. retail value $14.99) from *Tiger Electronics;* and a Sabrina, The Teenage Witch diary kit (approx. retail value $16.99) from *Pastime.* (approx. total retail value of prize package $3,000.00 for travel within the U.S. & Canada; £4,000 for travel from the U.K.) **Alternate grand prize:** In the event that the grand prize is unavailable, the following prize will be substituted: An Overnight Group Adventure at Apollo/Saturn V Center for three (winner plus friend and a parent or legal guardian). Winner and group will sleep under the Apollo/Saturn V rocket after an evening of space-related activities, including a Kennedy Space Center Visitor Complex group bus tour, pizza party dinner, a visit with Robot Scouts, hands-on activities. Winner and group will get a special NASA briefing of upcoming launches, demonstrations of Newton's Laws of Motion, midnight snack, breakfast, and 3-D IMAX film. Prize includes a commemorative certificate for each group and patch for each participant. If winner cannot take the trip on the specified date, the prize may be forfeited and an alternate winner may be selected.

Ten 1st Prizes: A Sabrina, The Teenage Witch Library (approx. retail value $150.00) from *Archway Paperbacks published by Pocket Books.* **Twenty 2nd Prizes:** A Sabrina, The Teenage Witch Gift Package including hand-held game (approx. retail value $14.99) from *Tiger Electronics,* diary kit (approx. retail value $16.99) from *Pastime,* Sabrina, The Teenage Witch CD-ROM (approx. retail value $29.99) from *Havas/SSI.* (approx. total retail value of prize package: $62.00). **Fifty 3rd Prizes:** A one-year Sabrina comic books subscription (approx. retail value $23.00) from *Archie Comics* and a Sabrina, The Teenage Witch diary kit (approx. retail value $16.99) from *Pastime* (Approx. total retail value of prize package $39.99.) The Grand Prize must be taken on the date specified by sponsors.

4. The sweepstakes is open to legal residents of the U.S., U.K. and Canada (excluding Quebec) ages 8–14 as of April 30, 2000, except as set forth below. Proof of age is required to claim prize. Prizes will be awarded to the winner's parent or legal guardian. Void in Puerto Rico and wherever prohibited or restricted by law. All federal, state, and local laws apply. Viacom International, Archie Comic Publications Inc., and the Kennedy Space Center Visitor Complex, their respective officers, directors, shareholders, employees, suppliers, parent companies, subsidiaries, affiliates, agencies, sponsors, participating retailers, and persons connected with the use, marketing or conduct of this sweepstakes are not eligible. Family members living in the same household as any of the individuals referred to in the preceding sentence are not eligible.

5. One prize per person or household. Prizes are not transferable and may not be substituted except by sponsors, in the event of prize unavailability, in which case the alternate grand prize outlined on previous page will be awarded. All prizes will be awarded. The odds of winning a prize depend upon the number of eligible entries received.

6. If a winner is a Canadian resident, then he/she must correctly answer a skill-based question administered by mail.

7. All expenses on receipt and use of prize including federal, state, and local taxes are the sole responsibility of the winners. Winners will be notified by mail. Winners may be required to execute and return an Affidavit of Eligibility and Publicity Release and all other legal documents which the sweepstakes sponsors may require (including a W-9 tax form) within 15 days of attempted notification or an alternate winner will be selected. The grand-prize winner's travel companions will be required to execute a liability release form prior to ticketing.

8. Winners or winners' parents on winners' behalf agree to allow use of their names, photographs, likenesses, and entries for any advertising, promotion, and publicity purposes without further compensation to or permission from the entrants, except where prohibited by law.

9. Winners and winners' parents or legal guardians, as applicable, agree that Viacom International, Inc., Archie Comic Publications Inc., and the Kennedy Space Center Visitor Complex, and their respective directors, shareholders, employees, suppliers, parent companies, subsidiaries, affiliates, agencies, sponsors, participating retailers, and persons connected with the use, marketing, or conduct of this sweepstakes, shall have no responsibility or liability for injuries, losses, or damages of any kind in connection with the collection, acceptance, or use of the prizes awarded herein, or from participation in this promotion.

10. By participating in this sweepstakes, entrants agree to be bound by these rules and the decisions of the judges and sweepstakes sponsors, which are final in all matters relating to the sweepstakes. Failure to comply with the Official Rules may result in a disqualification of your entry and prohibition of any further participation in this sweepstakes.

11. Names of major prize winners may be obtained (after May 31, 2000) by sending a stamped, self-addressed envelope to Prize Winners, Pocket Books "Sabrina, The Teenage Witch Space Launch Sweepstakes", 1230 Avenue of the Americas, 13th Floor, NY, NY 10020.